Beaten by a Balloon

To Ben and Luke – the boys next door   MM
To Tommy and Katherine   JBA

PUFFIN BOOKS
Published by the Penguin Group
Penguin Putnam Books for Young Readers, 345 Hudson Street, New York, New York 10014, U.S.A.
Penguin Books Ltd, 27 Wrights Lane, London W8 5TZ, England
Penguin Books Australia Ltd, Ringwood, Victoria, Australia
Penguin Books Canada Ltd, 10 Alcorn Avenue, Toronto, Ontario, Canada M4V 3B2
Penguin Books (N.Z.) Ltd, 182-190 Wairau Road, Auckland 10, New Zealand

Penguin Books Ltd, Registered Offices: Harmondsworth, Middlesex, England

First published in Great Britain by Hamish Hamilton Ltd, a division of Penguin Books Ltd, 1997
First published in the United States of America by Viking, a division of Penguin Books USA Inc., 1998
Published by Puffin Books, a member of Penguin Putnam Books for Young Readers, 2000

A Vanessa Hamilton Book

1 3 5 7 9 10 8 6 4 2

Text copyright © Margaret Mahy, 1997
Illustrations copyright © Jonathan Allen, 1997
All rights reserved

THE LIBRARY OF CONGRESS HAS CATALOGED THE VIKING EDITION UNDER CATALOG CARD NUMBER: 97-60373

Puffin Books ISBN 0-14-056666-X

Designed by Mark Foster
Printed in China

Beaten by a Balloon

Margaret Mahy

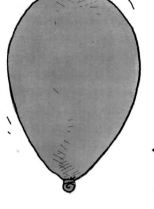

Illustrated by Jonathan Allen

PUFFIN BOOKS

"Dad," said Sam Appleby as they strolled down Snapper Street, "when we get home will you make me a sword?"

"A sword?" cried Mr Appleby. "Never! No violent toys in our family."

"But Dad," begged Sam, "Mr Mackie made Hacky Mackie a sword with a red jewel stuck on the handle. And Hacky's already got a plastic dagger, as well as a slingshot and a laser gun."

"Sam, I'm not giving you swords or laser guns, "said Mr Appleby sternly. "Your mother and I devote our lives to gentle, kindly things like ballooning, and growing roses and sunflowers. We hope you'll do the same."

"Oh, I like sunflowers and balloons," said Sam, "but I wouldn't mind having a sword as well."

"Hey! Appletree!" a mocking voice called out. And there was Hacky Mackie himself. He was prancing in front of his house, waving a sword in one hand, and a plastic laser space-gun in the other.

"I'm going to catch Buckbounder, the bank robber," yelled Hacky Mackie. "I'll win the reward and buy a photon cannon and shoot pieces off the moon. How about that, Appletree?"

And Hacky made the sound of a laser gun being fired over and over again at hideous aliens.

Mr Appleby ignored Hacky Mackie.

"I'll buy you a sunflower of your very own at the stall," he promised Sam.

The stall was on the corner of Gnashing Road and Cruncher Avenue. It sold almost everything – teddy bears, sunflowers, balloons, water pistols, red and white roses, pots of marmalade, and chocolate cakes.

"Dad," pleaded Sam, "couldn't I buy just one little water pistol?"

"No violent toys in our family!" said his father. "But you may

buy a balloon, and I will buy a chocolate cake for your mother, as well as the sunflower I promised you."

As the woman behind the stall handed Sam a beautiful sunflower in a terracotta pot, a mocking voice called, "Ha! Ha! Appletree!"

And there was Hacky Mackie, wandering past with his father. He aimed his laser gun at the sunflower.

"Stop that, Hacky!" said Mr Mackie with a smirk. "Poor people! You'll frighten them."

The woman in charge of the stall sold the Applebys a balloon, a sunflower and a chocolate cake. She also gave Sam a present of one red rose, its thorny stem wrapped in green tissue paper.

"Now you have a sunflower *and* a rose," said Mr Appleby, looking pleased. "But I've spent all my money. We'd better call in at the bank."

Turning into the Gnashing Road bank, Mr Appleby and Sam found themselves waiting in a long line.

Directly in front of them were Hacky Mackie and his father.
"Look, Dad! Two Appletrees!" said Hacky Mackie.
Mr Mackie looked over his shoulder and laughed.
Mr Appleby felt, just for a moment, that if only he had had a good plastic sword handy, he would soon have made Mr Mackie laugh on the other side of his face.

Suddenly, the door of the bank burst open.
"Hands up!" cried a rough voice.
"Ha! Ha! Ha! It is I, Buckbounder, and this is
a bank robbery."
Buckbounder bounced into the bank
waving his bank-robber's gun, and leaping
like a kangaroo on powerful springs welded
to the bottom of his boots. On these springs
he could bound across barriers and through
back gardens where no police paddy wagon
could go.

Give me all your money," he howled. "Give it to me *now*!"

Glancing scornfully at Sam's sunflower, he then turned to glare suspiciously at Hacky Mackie's laser gun.

Both Mackies wailed and fell to their knees.

Tearing the green tissue paper from the prickly rose stem, Sam moved quickly behind Buckbounder's back.

"Here's my watch and my parking-meter money," cried Mr Mackie. "Take them!"

"And here's my laser gun," wept Hacky Mackie. "Take it! Take it!"

At that moment, Sam thrust a thorn into his balloon. BANG! The balloon exploded right behind the bank robber.

BANG!

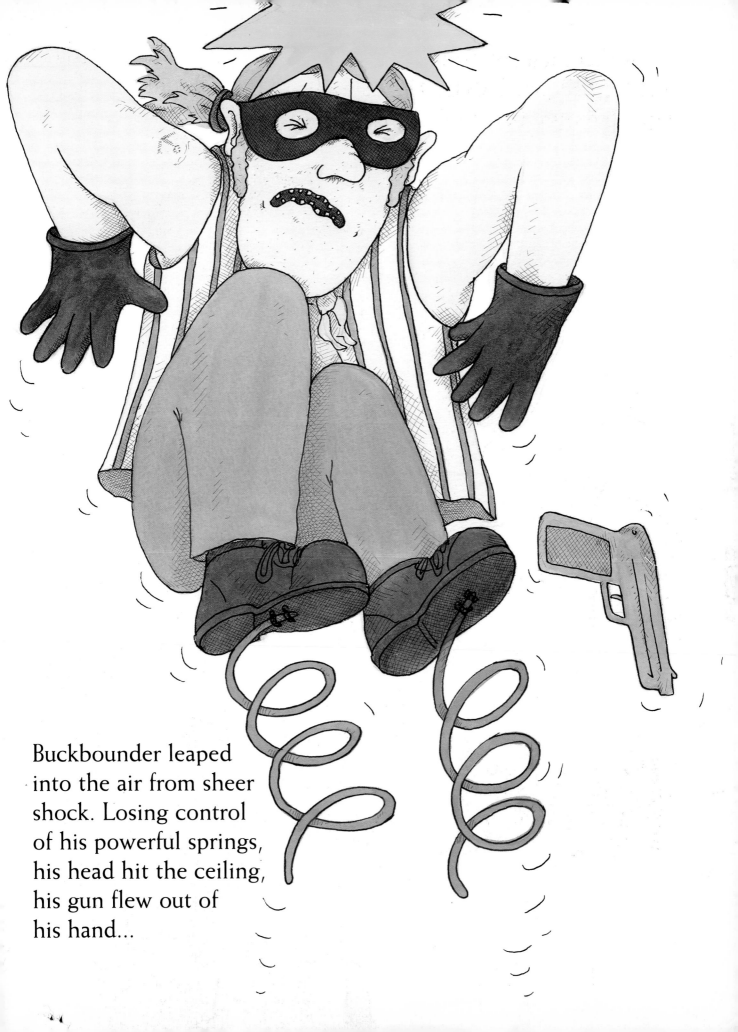

Buckbounder leaped
into the air from sheer
shock. Losing control
of his powerful springs,
his head hit the ceiling,
his gun flew out of
his hand...

...and he fell backwards with a painful thump. Mr Appleby promptly struck him in the face with the full force of the

chocolate cake. As Buckbounder writhed on the floor, blinded by icing, and with cake blocking his hairy nostrils,

Sam slid his sunflower out of the terracotta pot, and then jammed the pot over the villain's head, painfully pinching his large ears. While Buckbounder whooped and gasped, trying to get his head out of the pot and the cake out of his nose, the bank teller pressed the alarm button.

Two policemen, led by Sergeant Sidcup from the Gnashing Road Force (which happened to be right next door), rushed in with handcuffs.

Pulling the pot rather roughly off Buckbounder's head, Sergeant Sidcup passed it back to Sam.

"Brave boy! Brave boy!" he cried, shaking Sam's hand. "And you were quick-thinking, too, Sir. I could never have imagined such masterly assault by chocolate cake."

"We were only pretending to be terrified out of our wits!" cried Hacky Mackie, rising shakily from his knees. "Weren't we, Dad!"

"Never have I heard of anyone being so quick with a potted plant," Sergeant Sidcup said, ignoring the Mackies. "Re-pot that sunflower, Sir, keep it watered, and you'll be able to use it again if you are attacked by gangsters. And call in at the police station next door. We'll give you each a medal, and a large reward as well."

"Dad, *I* want a sunflower, too," Sam heard Hacky whining, as he and his father slunk out of the bank. But his father told him to shut up.

"Beaten by a balloon!" cried Buckbounder, as the two policemen swept him out of the bank. "Buckbounder beaten by a beastly balloon! I can't believe it."

"Dad, you were really violent with that chocolate cake. Does that mean a cake can be a dangerous weapon?" Sam asked his father in a puzzled voice next day.

Mr Appleby thought deeply, as fathers do.

"Well," he said, "I suppose it depends on who happens to be holding what and when. So perhaps, after all, I should buy you a small water pistol."

"Great!" cried Sam, grinning from ear to ear. "I'll use it to water my sunflower."